WELCOME TO
PASSPORT TO READING
A beginning reader's ticket to a brand-new world!

Every book in this program is designed to build read-along and read-alone skills, level by level, through engaging and enriching stories. As the reader turns each page, he or she will become more confident with new vocabulary, sight words, and comprehension.

These PASSPORT TO READING levels will help you choose the perfect book for every reader.

READING TOGETHER
Read short words in simple sentence structures together to begin a reader's journey.

READING OUT LOUD
Encourage developing readers to sound out words in more complex stories with simple vocabulary.

READING INDEPENDENTLY
Newly independent readers gain confidence reading more complex sentences with higher word counts.

READY TO READ MORE
Readers prepare for chapter books with fewer illustrations and longer paragraphs.

This book features sight words from the educator-supported Dolch Sight Words List. This encourages the reader to recognize commonly used vocabulary words, increasing reading speed and fluency.

For more information, please visit passporttoreadingbooks.com

Enjoy the journ

Little, Brown and Company

Hachette Book Group
237 Park Avenue, New York, NY 10017
Visit our website at lb-kids.com

Little, Brown and Company is a division of Hachette Book Group, Inc.
The Little, Brown name and logo are trademarks of Hachette Book Group, Inc.

The publisher is not responsible for websites (or their content) that are not owned by the publisher.

First Edition: August 2014

ISBN 978-0-316-33266-8

Library of Congress Control Number: 2014939548

10 9 8 7 6 5 4 3 2 1

CW

Printed in the United States of America

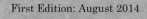

Passport to Reading titles are leveled by independent reviewers applying the standards developed by Irene Fountas and Gay Su Pinnell in *Matching Books to Readers: Using Leveled Books in Guided Reading,* Heinemann, 1999.

MEET THE BOXTROLLS™

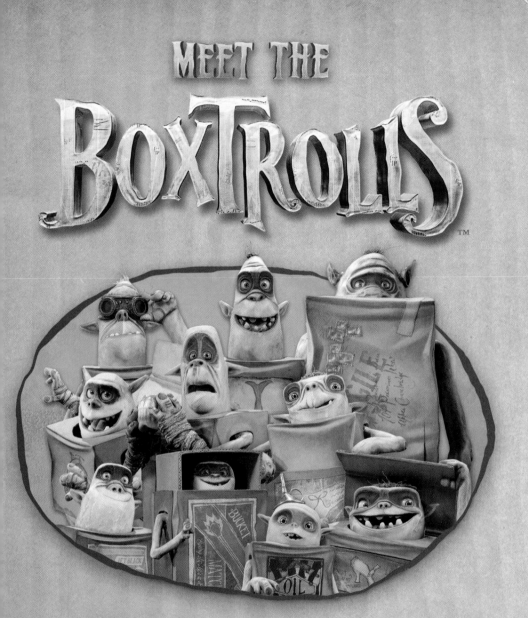

Adapted by Jennifer Fox
Screenplay by Irena Brignull & Adam Pava
Based upon the book *Here Be Monsters!* by Alan Snow

L B

LITTLE, BROWN AND COMPANY
New York   Boston

Attention, Boxtrolls fans!
Look for these words when you read
this book. Can you spot them all?

box

baby

underground

red hat

A group of boxes sits
in a dark alley.

One of them is special.
It is not just any box.

It is a Boxtroll named Fish!

"Gurgle, gurgle!" he says.

He hears a car and gets scared!
He goes underground.

Fish and his friends live
in a hidden world.
There are Shoe, Wheels,
Oil Can, and so many others!

Boxtrolls are gentle and kind.
They love to find and build things.

One of Fish's friends
looks different.
He is a human!

Eggs was a baby
and then grew up
with the Boxtrolls.

Eggs thinks he is one of them.

"I'm a Boxtroll!" he shouts.

Eggs is Fish's best friend.

> The Boxtrolls saved baby Eggs
> from the evil Mr. Snatcher.

Now Snatcher is trying
to catch the Boxtrolls.

Snatcher tells people that
Boxtrolls are evil monsters.
He is a liar.

"Lock your windows!
Bolt your doors!"
he shouts.

"Get them!" he tells
his gang of Red Hat goons—
Gristle, Trout, and Pickles.
Each goon wears a red hat.

There is a girl who does
not trust Snatcher.
Winnie Portley-Rind is
the mayor's daughter.

One day, she meets Eggs
and the Boxtrolls.

They become friends.
"Boxtrolls are not monsters,"
Winnie says.

She knows they have
big hearts.

Winnie and Eggs
must be brave to stop Snatcher
and his Red Hats.

They have to help
their Boxtroll friends.

"Do not be afraid!"

Eggs tells the Boxtrolls.

He makes them feel brave, too.

Now they are ready
to stop hiding and
to fight back.

Heroes come in all shapes and sizes!